RAGGEDY
ANN and ANDY
and the Kindly Ragman

RAGGEDY
ANN and ANDY
and the Kindly Ragman

JOHNNY GRUELLE

The Bobbs-Merrill Company, Inc.

Indianapolis · New York

1975

Printed in the United States of America
Designed by Viki Webb
Illustrated by John E. Hopper

The Little House of Teely Telly

"I think I hear the car pulling out," said Raggedy Ann.

"I'll go peek out of the window," Raggedy Andy said with a twinkle in his shoe-button eyes.

The two rag dolls were in the backyard doll house that Daddy had made out of a big wooden packing case. Mama and Daddy and Marcella were going away for a trip in the car. They were going to be gone the whole weekend. So the two rag dolls were planning to visit the Deep, Deep Woods full of elves and fairies and everything.

"Yes," said Raggedy Andy. "The car is pulling away. I can see Marcella in the back seat."

"Let's go to the Deep, Deep Woods and visit Teely Telly," said Raggedy Ann.

For, as you know, when the real-for-sure people are asleep or away, the dolls walk and talk and have all kinds of exciting adventures.

Teely Telly lived in the Deep, Deep Woods in a cunning little house hidden away down beneath the ferns, beside the huge trunk of a fallen tree.

Raggedy Ann and Andy often visited with Teely Telly when the real-for-sure people were asleep or away.

But now, when the two dolls reached Teely Telly's tiny house, their shoe-button eyes filled with tears, and great lumps came in their cottony throats. For, would you really and truly believe it, some mean creature had actually broken in the door of Teely Telly's lovely little home and had scattered her furniture all about.

"Well, well!" a kindly voice exclaimed, and the dolls looked up to see a man's cheery face peeping over the laurel at them. "How can you two look so glum on a lovely day like this?"

"Well, you see," Raggedy Andy said as the man walked up to the rag dolls, "someone has carried off our dear little Teely Telly!" And Raggedy Andy pointed to the little house beneath the ferns.

"Well, I'll declare!" the man cried. "Who could have done it?"

As the man walked closer to the tiny house he gave a cry of surprise, for he had suddenly shrunk in size until he was only twelve inches tall. "Dear me!" he exclaimed as he looked back at the two dolls who were now so large in comparison. "I guess I must be the smallest Ragman in the world! For that is what I am, you know, a Ragman."

"Teely Telly had a magic button with which she charmed a magic ring around her little house," Raggedy Ann explained to the Ragman. And as she and Raggedy

Andy walked near the house, they too became small. "She did that so whoever came near the place would be as small as she!"

The kindly Ragman led the way into Teely Telly's tiny house and saw the broken furniture scattered about. "Perhaps whoever did it wanted Teely Telly's magic button!" the Ragman said. "See!" He pointed out the back door. "There are footprints in the sand. Perhaps we can follow them and rescue Teely Telly!"

Just as the three friends walked out the back door, up came Buttons, a little pup dog that Raggedy Ann and Andy knew from Marcella's neighborhood. As he came up to the rag dolls, wagging his tail for all he was worth, he crossed through the magic ring around the house and he too became small.

The footprints through the sand and grass could easily be seen, and Buttons could follow the track by scent just as easily as could be.

And so, in a short time, our friends came to a strange

7

little tumbly shack which looked for all the world as if
it were about to fall over on its side and go to sleep.

As the Ragman and the dolls were about to pass the
tumbly shack, the top of a Dutch door swung open and
the head of a funny old woman peeped out. "Good morning!" she sang out in a cheery voice. "Won't you stop
awhile? I am Wamba the Witch, and I may be able to
help you!"

As the Ragman and the two dolls and little Buttons
walked into the funny little tumbly house, Wamba the
Witch said, "When I saw you coming down the path, I

looked into my magic mirror and saw just why you were so interested in looking at the ground! I'll show you the magic mirror so that you may see for yourself!" And she pulled back a curtain from one corner of the room, revealing a long mirror. "It is just like the magic mirror that belonged to Snow White," Wamba the Witch said.

Then she continued, "We will look in the magic mirror and see what we shall see!"

Then, as they sat and watched, our friends saw the little house of Teely Telly come into view. Three large men, their faces covered with whiskers, ran up to the door and broke it in. Then the three men came out of the back door carrying Teely Telly between them.

"I heard them pass my tumbly shack late last night!" Wamba the Witch said. "Now, watch in the magic mirror, and we shall see where they have taken Teely Telly."

The three men could be seen carrying Teely Telly between them down the path through the woods and into a cave. When they entered the cave, Wamba the Witch sighed. "It is strange," she said, "but the magic mirror does not show under the ground! We will have to follow them to the cave, and I can tell by my magic that we shall have a great many difficulties before we rescue Teely Telly."

"But we must follow the men and rescue Teely Telly," the Ragman said as he wiped a tear from his eye.

"By all means!" Wamba the Witch said. "Are you rag dolls brave enough to go?"

"Yes, indeed!" Both Raggedy Ann and Raggedy Andy replied. And little Buttons, just as if he had understood every word, jumped against the door and barked as if to say, "I'm ready. Let's hurry!"

"I will pack up a few things I wish to take," Wamba the Witch said.

She busied herself out in the kitchen and presently appeared carrying a tiny basket. Hanging from her belt was a little beaded pocketbook stuffed so full it looked like Santa Claus's stomach.

She carefully locked the front door and the back door and led the way to a little shed at the back of the house. From it she took four funny hobbyhorses made of broomsticks, each with a wooden horse's head at one end and two little spool wheels at the other.

"These will help us to cover the ground faster!" Wamba the Witch said. "All you have to do is straddle the hobbyhorses and lift your feet from the ground. He will take you as fast or as slow as you wish to go, and you can guide him by pulling on either rein."

So Wamba the Witch got upon her magic wooden hobbyhorse and, followed by the kindly Ragman and the Raggedys, sped away down the path in the direction taken by the men who had carried away Teely Telly.

Presently our friends came to a tumbling brook, and at a signal from Wamba the Witch they all got off their hobbyhorses and leaned them against a tree. Then Wamba the Witch took a tiny napkin from the little basket she carried and spread it upon the ground. The napkin grew and grew until it was a large tablecloth. Then Wamba the Witch mumbled a few magic words and the tablecloth was spread with good things to eat. There were sandwiches of all kinds, hard-boiled eggs, dill pickles, cakes and cookies, and everything one could wish for a picnic lunch.

Wamba the Witch, the Ragman, the Raggedys, and little Buttons were enjoying their magical picnic lunch so much that they did not notice a strange little man peep out from the bushes. Nor did they see him tiptoe quietly over to where the magic hobbyhorses leaned against a tree. The strange little man climbed upon one of the magical hobbyhorses and, holding the others by their reins, went sailing away down the path through the woods. Perhaps none of our friends would have discovered their loss until too late if Johnny Jaybird had not called out from a nearby tree, "Oh, Wamba the Witch, old Tunky has taken your hobbyhorses!"

The kindly Ragman sprang to his feet and ran after old Tunky, and Wamba the Witch and the two rag dolls ran behind the Ragman. But the magical hobbyhorses wheeled along so fast that the Raggedys, the Ragman

11

and their friends could not catch up, and, as they were out of breath, they had to stop to rest.

"Isn't that a shame?" Wamba the Witch cried. "Just when we needed the magical hobbyhorses the most!"

"It will delay us in our search for the men who carried away little Teely Telly!" the kindly Ragman said.

"I know just where old Tunky lives!" Johnny Jaybird cried as he hopped down upon the grass beside Wamba the Witch.

"Then we will have you show us the way to old Tunky's house, Johnny Jaybird," Wamba the Witch said.

So, with Johnny Jaybird perched upon Wamba's shoulder, our friends walked sadly down the path toward the home of mean old Tunky.

The Surrender of Mr. Tunky

Mean old Mister Tunky lived in a little house as funny looking as himself. It was a house built of sticks and stones and had one room built right on top of another, so Tunky's house was five stories high. Mean old Tunky had taken the magical hobbyhorses from Wamba the Witch and the kindly Ragman and Raggedy Ann and Raggedy Andy.

"Dear me!" Wamba the Witch cried as the four friends, with Buttons, the little pup dog, came up to old Tunky's queer house. "Tunky has gone inside and has locked the door! Now, how shall we ever get our hobby-horses so that we can follow the three men who carried away little Teely Telly?"

This was a question which the Ragman and the dolls could not answer, so they remained silent.

But old Tunky put his head out of the top window and laughed very rudely. "Ha, ha, ha!" he chuckled. "I

13

have always wanted one of your magical hobbyhorses, Wamba the Witch!" He made a face at the Ragman as he said this. "And now," he continued, "I not only have *one,* I have four. So when one wears out, I shall have another!"

"But, Mister Tunky," Raggedy Ann said, "it is very unkind of you to take our hobbyhorses just when we were trying so hard to catch up with the men who carried off little Teely Telly. We are very anxious to rescue Teely Telly."

"That may be quite true," old Mister Tunky replied. "But on the other hand, I am just as anxious to own the magical hobbyhorses! So you may as well run along and mind your own business." And with that, the mean old fellow closed the window with a bang, and our friends could hear him tramping about in the house.

"I suppose we are wasting time staying here," the Ragman said. "We shall never be able to get our hobbyhorses away from him while he is locked up inside his house."

"We might sit here until Tunky gets so hungry that he has to run to the grocery store for something to eat," Raggedy Ann suggested.

"But he might have enough food in his house to last a week!" Raggedy Andy said.

"I could easily work magic upon his food and spoil it," Wamba the Witch said. "But that would be unkind, and even though Tunky has been unkind to us, that is no reason why we should be unkind to him."

"That is quite true, Wamba," the kindly Ragman said, "and you have a very kindly heart."

14

"Perhaps you might work your magic upon the hobby-horses and make them break through the door of Tunky's funny house," Raggedy Ann suggested.

Wamba the Witch laughed. "Quite an idea, my dear! I shall try it."

So, getting out her little beaded bag, Wamba the Witch spread all of her magical charms in a circle upon the ground and then hopped about the circle singing a strange magical song.

When Wamba the Witch had finished her magical song, everything was quiet for a moment; then there

was a loud scuffling and then a number of hard thumps on the door of Tunky's house.

"Whee!" Raggedy Andy cried as he jumped about in his excitement. "The magical hobbyhorses are trying to break down the door!"

Mean old Mister Tunky added his voice to the din, yelling loudly for the hobbyhorses to stand still and trying his best to keep out of their way as they rolled madly about his little room.

But, although Wamba the Witch's magic worked quite well, it did not work well enough for the magical hobbyhorses to batter down Tunky's door. And for fear that the magical hobbyhorses might break off their wooden heads and so become useless, Wamba the Witch had to work her magic again to quiet them.

"I guess mean old Tunky has built his house very strongly," Wamba the Witch said. "We might as well run along and try to rescue little Teely Telly without the magical hobbyhorses."

"There must be some way to get into Tunky's house," Raggedy Andy said. "If we cannot break in the door, perhaps we may be able to get in some other way," and he walked around the queer house to see if he could find a way to climb to the upper windows.

When Raggedy Andy returned to where his friends were seated, he said, "There is a long ladder at the back of the house, and I am sure we can put it up to one of the windows and climb inside."

Old Mister Tunky poked his head out of one of the windows and laughed. "Don't you believe it!" he cried. "I can hear every word you say, and I know just what you intend to do. So I shall double-bar every window, and I know you will never be able to get inside! You may as well run on home to your mothers, because you shall never, never get the magical hobbyhorses!" And again he banged the window shut, and our friends could hear the mean creature running from one floor to another, barring the windows.

"Oh, I know what let's do!" Raggedy Andy said.

"What shall we do?" Wamba the Witch, the Ragman and Raggedy Ann wanted to know as they crowded about Raggedy Andy.

"I can hear every word you say!" Tunky howled again from his keyhole.

"I want you to hear everything I say!" Raggedy Andy replied with a twinkle in one shoe-button eye. "Then you will understand why it will be best for you to give us our magical hobbyhorses."

"I shall never agree to that!" Old Tunky howled.

"You all can see," Raggedy Andy explained, "that mean old Mister Tunky's house is right at the bottom of a hill. And, if you look up the hill, you will see a lot of large boulders. Now, if we go up the hill and roll some of the large boulders down against Tunky's house, they will smash his house to bits, and we shall find the magical hobbyhorses in the wreckage." And Raggedy Andy winked his left eye slowly and held up one cotton-stuffed hand to show that he really did not mean what he said.

As old Mister Tunky could not see Raggedy Andy wink, he really thought Raggedy Andy meant to be that unkind, so he opened a window and howled, "If you do that, you know you will be very unkind, and even though I may have been unkind to you, that is no sign you should be unkind to me! That is what Wamba the Witch just said a minute ago."

"You wait and see," the kindly Ragman replied. "Or, better still, open the door and put the magical hobby-horses out on your doorstep!"

And with that, our friends walked up the hill until they came to the large stones. "Here's a nice one!" Raggedy Andy said, winking again. "And we can easily pry it loose so that it will roll down against old Tunky's house and crash it all to pieces."

So he pushed and pulled on the large stone, and the others helped until it finally began to move. All together, our friends rocked the stone back and forth as if they were really trying to start it rolling.

Mean old Tunky, watching from his window, howled ever so loudly as he saw the stone move. "Don't roll it," he cried. "I will give you one of the magical hobby-horses!"

"All of them or none!" the kindly Ragman cried in reply. And as he said this, he unintentionally pushed too hard upon the large stone and it began rolling, slowly at first, then faster and faster down the hill, straight toward the queer house of mean little old Tunky.

"Stop it! Stop it!" Tunky screamed from his window as he watched the stone come bouncing and crashing toward him. "I will gladly give you all of your magical hobbyhorses!"

Wamba the Witch barely had time to feel in her beaded bag and rub one of her charms to try to keep the

large stone from striking Tunky's house squarely at the front door.

In fact, she and all the others shut their eyes so as not to see Tunky's house fly to pieces. There was a loud crash and the sound of flying wood. As our friends looked, they saw that the large stone, through the magic of Wamba, had barely missed the house but had carried away one corner of Tunky's woodshed.

Scarcely had the echoes of the crash died before the front door flew open and mean little Tunky ran out, pulling the magical hobbyhorses by their bridles. "Here, take them!" he screamed. "And I hope you never bring them by here again!"

Wamba the Witch laughed. "We hope that, if we do, we shall find you in a better temper. When anyone has been as mean as you have been, they cloud up their lives so darkly, they cannot find happiness in anything!" And as she and her friends hopped upon the magical hobby-horses, she added to Tunky, "When people cannot find happiness in such a beautiful world as this, it is simply because they have closed the windows to their hearts and shut out all of the sunshine of happiness."

The Wind-Up Land Pirates

"I do hope we shall soon overtake the mean men who captured Teely Telly and carried her away!" Raggedy Andy said as he and Raggedy Ann, the kindly Ragman and Wamba the Witch rode through the woods on the witch's magical hobbyhorses. Little Buttons the pup dog ran gaily along beside his friends, wagging his stubby tail and barking happily at every strange thing he saw.

"We have been delayed so long by mean old Mister Tunky taking the magical hobbyhorses, I am afraid the mean men have gotten far ahead of us," the kindly Ragman said.

After a while, the magical hobbyhorses carried our friends out of the woods and onto a great plain. For a short distance, the path leading from the woods could be followed, but soon it grew more indistinct, and finally there was no telling which way Teely Telly had been taken.

Presently, upon arriving at a hilltop, Raggedy Andy, who was in the lead, held up his cotton-stuffed hand for everyone to stop. There, across the valley, looking like specks in the distance, could be seen a camp and figures of people moving about.

"It must be the camp of the mean men who captured little Teely Telly," the kindly Ragman said.

Raggedy Andy called to Buttons, but the little dog was so intent upon following the scent of the men that he either did not hear or would not hear. There was really nothing to do but follow, catch Buttons, and trust that the men had not seen them at this distance. So our friends cried to their magical hobbyhorses and went racing after Buttons, who by now had disappeared over a small hill.

Just as Raggedy Andy, Raggedy Ann, Wamba the Witch and the kindly Ragman raced through a narrow place in the hill, six wild-looking pirates jumped out and caught the bridles of the magical hobbyhorses and brought them to a stop. "Oh, dear!" Raggedy Ann cried. "Now we are captured as well as little Teely Telly. What shall we do? We are captured by pirates! And they must be *land* pirates, at that!"

One of the land pirates took Wamba the Witch's bag of magical charms from her. Looking inside it, he found nothing which he considered of value, so he tossed it into the bushes.

"Oh dear!" Wamba the Witch sighed, disappointed that the bag was not returned to her. "Now we are indeed lost!"

"Cheer up!" the kindly Ragman consoled her. "One is

22

never lost while there is the least bit of hope. I have discovered one thing: I do not believe the pirates can understand us!"

"And they are land pirates!" cried Raggedy Andy. "But they look just like the ones you see in the pictures in storybooks about the olden days on the sea. Except they're made out of metal. Almost like toy pirates."

"What are they talking about?" one pirate asked another.

"I can't understand a word they say," the other pirate replied.

"Why, they can talk!" Raggedy Ann cried. "They talk just as well as we do!"

All this time, the land pirates had been taking our friends toward the camp; upon arriving there, the pirate captain and all the other pirates came crowding about.

"I see you have captured them," the captain cried as he rubbed his metal hands together. "Did they offer much resistance?"

"We captured them as easy as pie, O great Captain Bandanna," replied the pirate who held Raggedy Andy's magical hobbyhorse.

"We wish you would let us go," Wamba the Witch said to the land pirate captain. "We are not bothering you, and we are in search of Teely Telly!"

"They do not speak our language," the metal pirate said to Captain Bandanna. "What shall we do with them?"

"Better put them in the animal cage until after dinner. Then we shall determine what to do."

"Aren't they blockheads?" Raggedy Andy cried. "We

talk the same as they do, but they think that because they are metal pirates and we are not, we talk a strange language!"

"As long as they think that, it is just as well," the Ragman said. "For then we can plan a way to escape and they will not understand what we plan!"

"Just the same," Wamba the Witch said, "we had better not plan while they can hear us, for they may understand and just be pretending they don't."

The land pirates pushed Wamba the Witch, the kindly Ragman and the children into a wooden cage

and locked the door. Then they gathered around the Captain and waited to hear what he might have to say.

"We will talk of the situation while we have dinner!" Captain Bandanna cried as he struck his metal hands together. At this signal, ten pirates came running out with boxes and oil cans and placed them in front of the captain and the other pirates.

"I do believe they are eating metal filings!" Raggedy Ann cried as the pirates dug their hands into the boxes.

"What do they say, O brave Jolly Roger?" Captain Bandanna asked of the pirate who had captured Raggedy Andy.

"I cannot understand, O great Captain Bandanna!" Roger replied. "But I believe they want some of our food."

"Oil me up a little, Roger," Captain Bandanna said, "so that I may better think what to do with our captives."

The land pirate named Jolly Roger took the oil can and oiled a hole in the top of Captain Bandanna's head. Then he oiled his arms, his knees and every joint of his metal body. Then, when he had finished, he and the other metal pirates took oil cans and oiled themselves.

"I can think ever so much better!" Captain Bandanna said. "I know what we'll do. We will blindfold our captives at daylight and make them walk the plank!"

"Aha!" all the metal pirates cried as they hopped up and danced about.

"Silence!" Captain Bandanna cried. "As it is daylight now, we put the blindfolds on right away!"

At this, four of the metal pirates ran to their tin tents and came out with four colorful bandanna handkerchiefs. The land pirates placed the handkerchiefs over the eyes of Raggedy Ann, Raggedy Andy, the kindly Ragman, and Wamba the Witch. "Bring them over to the plank," the pirate captain cried.

"They are ready and lined up!" the pirate named Jolly Roger replied.

"Prepare to walk the plank!" Captain Bandanna cried.

"My country, 'tis of thee," Raggedy Andy began singing with his head held high. Raggedy Ann, the kindly Ragman, and Wamba the Witch joined in, and they sang the song to its end.

The pirate captain, surprised at this show of bravery, did not give the command to walk until after the song was finished and the kindly Ragman had turned and whispered hurriedly to his friends.

"Steady now!" Captain Bandanna commanded. "Walk! Three! Four!"

And one by one our friends walked to the end of the plank. And Raggedy Ann, Raggedy Andy, Wamba the Witch and the kindly Ragman tumbled to the ground.

"There! That's finished!" Captain Bandanna cried as he got up and walked back toward the metal tents, followed by all the metal pirates.

Raggedy Andy, Raggedy Ann, Wamba the Witch, and the kindly Ragman lay just as they had fallen, while the pirates gathered around their captain.

The captain gave a command and a metal pirate came running out with a large metal key. This he put in the back of the pirate captain and wound him up. Then

he went around to all the other pirates and wound them up. "Now we can sleep for two hours," Captain Bandanna said as he stretched himself upon the ground. "We are certain not to run down before we wake up."

Presently all the land pirates began snoring, and it sounded just like a metal buzz saw. "What did I tell you?" The kindly Ragman laughed softly as he sat up and brushed off the dust. "I knew the end of that plank was just a foot off the ground. We couldn't have been hurt."

"After you whispered to us, I remembered I had seen it too!" Raggedy Andy said.

"Now that the wind-up pirates are fast asleep, we had better make our escape," Wamba the Witch suggested.

"While you three run away across the field, I will tiptoe up and see if I can get our magical hobbyhorses," Raggedy Andy said.

"That is a good idea," the kindly Ragman said. "Wamba, you and Raggedy Ann hold hands and run as fast as you can. And while Raggedy Andy goes after the magical hobbyhorses, I will run back to where we

were captured and find your bag of magical charms!"

So Wamba the Witch caught hold of Raggedy Ann's soft cotton-stuffed hand and away they ran across the field. "My! I was a little bit frightened!" Raggedy Ann said when she and Wamba the Witch stopped to rest.

"And it just goes to show, too, that one should not permit himself to be frightened," Wamba laughed. "For, had we all been frightened, the kindly Ragman might not have noticed how low to the ground the plank was. If they had heard our voices coming from such a short distance, there is no telling what the wind-up pirates might have done to us afterward!"

"Here comes Raggedy Andy with the magical hobby-horses," Raggedy Ann said.

"And I see the kindly Ragman has my bag of magical charms," said Wamba the Witch, delighted. "Now we are safe!"

Another Adventure with the Wind-Up Pirates

Raggedy Ann, Raggedy Andy, Wamba the Witch, and the kindly Ragman were grateful for having escaped from the band of wind-up land pirates.

"It is indeed fortunate that their gangplank was only a foot off the ground," the kindly Ragman said as he came up to Wamba and the rag dolls.

"And now that the land pirates are fast asleep, let us hurry away before they discover they did not really and truly kill us," Raggedy Ann said.

"Well, I have our magical hobbyhorses," Raggedy Andy said, "so let us ride away and see if we can discover where our little pup dog Buttons has gone."

"I am sure that little Buttons circled around the camp of the wind-up pirates and is still following the trail of the three wicked men who are carrying little Teely Telly away," Wamba the Witch said.

So our friends climbed upon their magical hobbyhorses and were just about to start when they heard ahead of them the shouts of eight wind-up pirates. These pirates had evidently been hunting and were returning to camp with two metal deer.

The pirates surrounded our friends and marched them back to the pirate camp and awakened Captain Bandanna and his crew.

"Dear me!" Captain Bandanna cried as he sat up and rubbed his eyes. "How does it happen that you have our captives when we just finished making them walk the plank a few moments ago?"

"I do not know, O great Captain Pirate Bandanna," one of the wind-up buccaneers replied. "Whenever we make any of our wind-up captives walk the plank, they never get up and run away. Maybe these strange people, not being fine wind-up beings as we are, do not know how to play!"

"Well," the pirate captain mused, "it will do no good making them walk the plank over again, so let's put them back in the wooden cage until I can think of some other punishment for them."

So, with a wave of his hand, the pirate captain motioned for Raggedy Ann and Raggedy Andy, Wamba the Witch, and the kindly Ragman to be taken to the cage and locked up. Then, with a large metal yawn, the captain and his followers again rolled themselves up in metal blankets and were soon fast asleep.

"Do you suppose Buttons is still chasing after the men who captured little Teely Telly?" Raggedy Andy asked after a while.

As if in answer to his question, little Buttons slipped

31

around one of the tents, walking as quietly as he could.

"He's looking for us," Wamba the Witch whispered. "No, he isn't!" she decided. "He's going into the tent from which the land pirates brought the oil cans and the metal filings for the pirates' dinner!"

"Look! He's coming out! Run, Buttons! Run!" Raggedy Ann cried.

At the sound of Raggedy Ann's cry, the wind-up pirates sprang to their feet and looked about. Two pirates with long sticks started running after little Buttons. The others joined in the chase, but Buttons dodged

this way and that and ran lickety-split past the cage and across the plain.

"Well, we can't catch him," the land pirate captain said as he walked back and took a seat beside the wooden cage. "And besides, we don't want him anyway!"

"Oh yes we do, O great Captain Bandanna!" one of the pirates cried. "That puppy dog has taken the key, and I shall be unable to wind anyone up until we recover it!"

"Then we must chase the puppy dog and recover the key!" Captain Bandanna cried. "After him, men, and do not return until you have captured him. I am beginning to feel right now as if I were running down!"

All of the storybook pirates now started out in pursuit of little Buttons.

"If my men don't catch your little dog, we will soon run down," the pirate captain said. "And if we run down, there will be no one to unlock the cage, and you will stay there forever and ever and ever a-n-d e-v-e-r-a-n-d e---v---e---" his voice grew fainter and slower until our friends could hear only a whirring like the wheels of a big old-fashioned grandfather clock before it strikes. The pirate captain turned around once, slowly, and then with a little clicking sound fell to the ground.

"There!" Raggedy Ann cried. "He has run down! All the pirates have run down by this time and we shall never be rescued."

"Oh," said Wamba the Witch, "I almost feel like crying," and Raggedy Ann put her arms about her shoulders and kissed her kindly. "But I know that, in the first place, it does no good to cry. And in the second place, it makes your eyes and nose red and you are not so pretty then."

Raggedy Andy tried kicking the wooden door to the cage but soon gave up, for all he could do was to make the door rattle, and this did not help anything.

"Aha!" the kindly Ragman cried after a while. "Here comes Buttons, and there are three of the wind-up pirates after him. Evidently they had better wind-up springs than the captain."

"They are not running very fast," Raggedy Andy said. "Little Buttons is running just fast enough to keep ahead of them! I'll bet a nickel they are almost run down, too."

"Yes! There goes one of them!" Raggedy Ann cried as one of the pirates tumbled to the ground.

"And there goes another!" the kindly Ragman cried.

"Here, Buttons! Here, Buttons!" Raggedy Andy cried. "Here, boy!"

Little Buttons did not run any faster but continued toward the cage, and our friends could see that he still carried the key in his mouth. He ran around the wooden cage three times, with the metal pirate staggering after him. Then, the fourth time, when Buttons came around in front of the cage he sat down, and the prisoners knew that the land pirate's wind-up works had run down and that he had tumbled to the ground in back of the cage.

"That was the finest chase I ever had in my life,"

little Buttons said as he dropped the metal key to the ground and wagged his tail.

"Why, Buttons can talk!" Raggedy Andy cried in excitement.

"I have always talked," the puppy replied.

"Perhaps you have, Buttons," Raggedy Ann said, "but you have never talked anything except puppy-dog language before."

"Well, it seems just the same to me," Buttons replied.

"Now, how shall we get out?" Raggedy Ann wanted to know. "All the wind-up pirates have run down and cannot unlock the door to this cage."

"Did you notice where they put the key to the door?" Buttons asked.

"I saw the captain put it in his pocket," the Ragman said.

Little Buttons walked over and pulled and tugged at the captain's pocket until he pulled the key out; then, by standing on his hind feet and holding the key up,

the pup was able to get it within reach of the Ragman's fingers.

It took only a moment for the Ragman to unlock the door.

"Now we must find our magical hobbyhorses and make our escape," Wamba said.

So she took the key to the land pirates' wind-up works and, picking up Buttons, gave the word. Then, riding their magic hobbyhorses, they all sailed away across the plain until they came to the pirate who was farthest from his camp. Then Wamba, advising the others to be ready to ride away, got off her hobbyhorse and, placing the key in the back of the metal pirate, wound him up.

As the pirate came to life, Wamba the Witch stepped back and threw the key as far as she could in the direction of the pirate camp. "Now," she said to the pirate, "run and get the key and hasten to your captain! All of your friends have run down and they will need to be wound up so that they in turn can wind you more." And as the pirate ran toward the key, Wamba the Witch jumped upon her magical hobbyhorse and, followed by her friends, went lickety-split across the plain toward a woods in the distance.

The Ice Cream Mud Puddle

When Wamba the Witch threw the key toward the land pirates' camp, she, Raggedy Ann and Andy, and the kindly Ragman hopped upon their magical hobby-horses and rode away as fast as they could go.

"When you left us, where did you go, little Buttons?" Wamba the Witch asked the little pup dog.

"Why," Buttons replied, "I was following the scent of the three men who captured our dear friend, little Teely Telly."

"Did you follow their trail in this direction?" Raggedy Ann asked.

"I followed their trail as far as those two hills ahead of us," Buttons said. "Then, when I looked back, I saw that you had been captured by the wind-up pirates, and I turned back to see if I could help you."

When our friends had ridden along for a few minutes in silence, Buttons said, "Now we are getting to the place where I turned around and saw you captured by the pirates. Perhaps you had better put me to the ground, Wamba, so I can tell in which direction the trail of the three wicked men runs!"

"I guess that would be a good idea," Wamba said as she brought her magical hobbyhorse to a stop and let Buttons jump to the ground.

Little Buttons made a large circle, running as fast as he could go, then headed away. "This is their trail," he called back.

Buttons, of course, could not run as fast as the magical hobbyhorses could go, so our friends had to slow the hobbyhorses to follow little Buttons until he came to a queer little house.

Buttons ran all around the house and then to the door. "The trail of the three men who captured little Teely Telly leads right to the door of this little house," the pup said.

"Oh, Buttons, you must be mistaken!" Raggedy Ann said. "The house is too small to hold Teely Telly and three large men."

"Just the same, I cannot find their trail leading anywhere except up to the door."

"Then we had better go inside and see if they are really there," Raggedy Andy said.

So Raggedy Andy knocked upon the door with his soft cotton-stuffed hand, and someone inside asked, "Who is tapping on my door? Who is tapping more and more?"

"It's us," Raggedy Andy said in reply.

"Then I shall not let us in, for my house is in a muss," the voice inside sang.

39

"Well, then, perhaps you will come out?" the kindly Ragman suggested.

"Ah! I never thought of that; wait until I get my hat. I am Stiles, the stilt maker," the little man said. "And the last three pairs of stilts I made, the three men walked away without so much as saying, 'Thank you.'"

"Did they have a lovely little fairylike creature with them by the name of Teely Telly?" Wamba the Witch asked Stiles.

"That I cannot say," Stiles replied. "I saw only the one who took the three pairs of stilts; for, when I handed them to him, he gave me such an ugly scowl, I hastened to shut the door and bolt it."

"Then that is why I could not track them farther than Stiles's front porch," little Buttons said.

"I heard three men talking, though," Stiles said.

"Thank you ever so much, Mr. Stiles," Wamba the Witch said. "No doubt, those three men are the ones we are seeking."

It was easy, now that our friends knew the three men had walked away upon stilts. Each step they had taken had punched a hole in the ground.

Led by Wamba the Witch, our friends followed the stilt tracks away from the house into a thick woods. After going a short way, Wamba gave a cry. "Here are the stilts!" she said as her friends came up to her. "Evidently the three men know that we are following them and have taken off the stilts to throw us off their track."

"I can easily follow them now," Buttons said as he started down a path.

The path led close beside a tinkling brook, and before

long our friends came to a sign which read, "To the Ice Cream Mud Puddle," and there was a finger on the sign which pointed the direction.

Wamba the Witch laughed. "I've read of ice cream mud puddles, but I never knew they were really and truly for sure."

"Let us follow the sign and enjoy some of the wild ice cream!" the kindly Ragman laughed.

So, following in the direction in which the finger pointed, our friends soon came to a round base in which chocolate ice cream bubbled up just like custard pud-

ding does when Marcella's Mama cooks it for Marcella. At the side of the base were little wooden plates and wooden spoons, all nice and new.

Raggedy Andy and the kindly Ragman had just started to help Wamba the Witch and Raggedy Ann to a dish of the chocolate ice cream when a great voice cried, "Aha! So now I know who it is that has been taking my ice cream," and walking toward them came a ferocious fat man waving a large stick in his hand.

"But we have never been here before," the kindly Ragman said. "And we did not know that you owned the ice cream mud puddle. We are sorry."

"Indeed! I intend to make you feel sorry," the large man cried as he walked up and swung his stick at the head of the kindly Ragman.

The Ragman ducked his head just in time to escape, but the blow sent his hat flying. As the large man started to strike again, little Buttons nipped his ankle. My! How

42

the large man howled and danced about, trying to strike little Buttons! This gave the kindly Ragman time to run into the woods and cut a long stick for himself. Then, without the least show of fear, although the mean man was ever so much larger than he, the kindly Ragman, with a smile on his face, walked close, and as the big man struck at him, the Ragman deftly caught the blow upon the side of his stick. Each time the large man struck, the kindly Ragman turned the blow aside.

This made the big man so angry that he made the woods ring with his cries, so that Raggedy Ann and Wamba the Witch had to hold their hands over their ears, or at least Wamba did, for Raggedy Ann didn't really have any ears, but she put her hands up anyway.

When the kindly Ragman had turned aside forty or fifty of the blows, a little man with a peaked cap walked up and laughed. "Ha, ha, ha! Now, old Meany, here is someone smaller than yourself who is not afraid and who will not be driven away from the ice cream!"

The little man turned to Wamba the Witch and continued, "Old Meany drives every small creature away from the ice cream mud puddle, and it doesn't belong to him at all."

"And I'll drive these people away, too, just as soon as I can hit this man one good blow upon the head!" old Meany cried as he redoubled his efforts and swung his stick at the kindly Ragman.

This seemed to arouse the kindly Ragman, and the smile faded from his face. He danced about more cautiously, and when an opening came, he brought his

stick down so hard upon the large man's head that the stick flew to pieces.

Old Meany's legs sagged under him and he sat down with a hard thump and rolled over and over, holding the top of his head with both hands. The strange little man ran and caught up old Meany's stick and was about to give him another crack when the kindly Ragman stopped him.

"If you knew him as well as I, you would let me give just eight or ten hard cracks upon his head," the little man said. "He really deserves it!"

But the kindly Ragman took Meany's stick and said to the little man, "Then it is all right for us to have some of the ice cream?"

"Yes, indeed! The ice cream mud puddle was made by a fairy princess for all of us. Old Meany drives everyone away."

"I shall never fight with you again," old Meany cried to the Ragman. "I'll run home and put vinegar and brown paper on my head. That's what I'll do."

The kindly Ragman helped Wamba and Raggedy Ann to dishes of ice cream, while Raggedy Andy helped the strange little man to a dish.

The Ragman laughed. "Now that that is all over, let's enjoy ourselves! For, no matter how cloudy the skies may seem, afterward the sun always seems to shine the brightest, and we need storms the better to enjoy the sunshine."

"How true, indeed," Wamba the Witch said. "If it weren't for the storms, we would never see the beautiful rainbows!"

A Fairy Castle Disappears

Wamba the Witch, the kindly Ragman, the Raggedys, little Buttons the puppy, and the strange little man sat beside the ice cream mud puddle in the woods eating the magic ice cream. "It is the nicest ice cream I have ever tasted," Raggedy Andy said when he had eaten three dishes.

"You promised to tell us about old Meany and also about the three wicked men who carried away our dear little friend Teely Telly," Raggedy Ann reminded the little man.

"Perhaps I might best start way back when the mud puddle was first made." The little man puffed on his pipe and blew three rings into the air, then continued, "My name is Loody and I have lived in a little stone house a short way from here for years and years—more years than I would dare tell you for fear you might doubt my word. And long, long ago there used to be a lovely castle standing by the side of a lake, right near the center of this forest. I saw the castle many times, though I never ventured inside the large gate.

"The castle was owned by the fairy princess who made this lovely ice cream mud puddle. Indeed, the fairy princess made a number of very magical things here in the forest for the forest people.

"But one day as I passed the lake, I was standing, looking across at the castle and thinking how beautiful it was, all of white and pink marble there in the sunshine, with its tall towers and turrets reaching almost to the clouds, when—what do you think?" Loody pointed his pipestem from one to the other of his listeners.

"Well, sir," Loody sighed, "as I looked, a large black cloud settled about the fairy castle; thunder popped and rumbled; then, when the black cloud faded away, the lovely, beautiful castle of the fairy princess had disappeared.

"While I had never been fortunate enough to see the fairy princess, there are others living here in the forest who saw and talked with her, and they have told me what a beautiful being she was."

"And no one has seen the fairy princess since the day her fairy castle disappeared?" the kindly Ragman asked.

"No one," Loody replied sadly.

"Hmmmm!" Wamba the Witch mused. "There is no doubt but that the fairy princess and her lovely castle were done away with through powerful magic. I wish we could see the place. Perhaps with my magic charms I might be able to find out just what happened."

"Maybe old Meany had something to do with it," the kindly Ragman suggested.

"Oh, no!" little Loody laughed. "Old Meany has lived near here as long as I can recollect, and he has always been just the same. He is selfish and disagreeable, but he does not know the first thing about working magic. I have talked with him about the fairy castle, but he does not know as much about it as I, for he did not see it disappear as I did."

"You promised to tell us of old Meany and the three men," Raggedy Andy reminded Loody.

"I had not forgotten," Loody laughed good-naturedly, "and I was just about to tell you, but really, when I get to thinking of the lovely fairy castle, it makes me heart-sick. It was lovely! I wish you could have seen it."

"We wish so too," Raggedy Ann and the others said together. "It must have been very beautiful."

"It was indeed," Loody said. "Well, as I said before, old Meany has always lived near here; but as long as the princess lived in the fairy castle, old Meany did not drive anyone away from the ice cream mud puddle, for I am certain that the beautiful fairy princess would have known of it and would have prevented him from keeping persons from enjoying it. But when old Meany found that the fairy castle had disappeared and the princess with it, he started calling the ice cream mud puddle his and driving all of us away from it. When I came here a short time before you friends came, I heard loud words. So I peeped through the bushes and saw three large men sitting here eating ice cream.

"They had a box," Loody continued, "and I am certain that something very valuable was in the box, for one of the men kept one hand on it all the time. I saw old Meany come running through the woods, and I knew that he intended driving the people away from the ice cream mud puddle. But when he came running out here in the open and discovered the three large fierce-looking men, he stopped so suddenly his feet flew out from under him and he almost slid into the ice cream mud puddle. The three men were surprised at first. One reached and picked up the box, while the others drew their swords. But, seeing only old Meany,

the largest man, who seemed to be the leader, put his sword away and gave old Meany a cuff on his head."

"Old Meany scooted for home, I'll bet!" said Raggedy Ann with a soft cottony chuckle.

"Which way did the three men go?" Wamba the Witch asked. "You know, we are following them and shall try and rescue little Teely Telly, the Raggedys' little friend!"

"I can show you the way they went," Loody promised, "but I would advise you to be very careful. They are large, fierce, strong, wicked-looking men, all armed with swords. I am certain you will be unable to rescue your little friend Teely Telly as you are. You will need at least two other men to help the kindly Ragman fight; and, even then, the three men have swords, and the Ragman has only a stick."

"If we can catch up with them, I shall fight all three," the kindly Ragman said, "swords or no swords!"

The kindly Ragman got to his feet and offered a hand to Wamba the Witch and Raggedy Ann. "If you will kindly show us which way the three men went, we will follow," the Ragman said as he whirled old Meany's stout stick about his head.

"I shall be glad to show you," Loody agreed. "And you will be surprised, too, I'll bet, when you see where they went."

With little Buttons scampering in front, Loody led the others through the woods until they came to a lake. Around the edge of the lake ran a path. "It was here that I stood and saw the castle of the fairy princess disappear," Loody said as he pointed across the water. "And there, where you see the trees the thickest, is

51

where the beautiful castle stood. We will follow the path around the lake," he added, "but I would advise that we keep as still as possible."

When Loody led the way almost to where the fairy castle had stood, he left the path and made a circle into the woods. When he stopped, he whispered, "The three men with the box left the path there and must have gone through the briars and thorns, for I saw them no more. And," he added, "if you will take my advice, you will turn about and return home, for I have tried time and again to find a way through the briars and thorns but have never been able to go more than a few feet. And now," he said, as he shook hands with the kindly Ragman, Wamba the Witch and the Raggedys, "I must leave you. You had best follow me back."

"Thank you so much," Wamba the Witch said. "We shall stay here and at least talk it over."

The Fairy Castle Is Found

"If the three men who captured little Teely Telly went through the thicket of briars and thorns, as Mr. Loody told us they did, there must be a path there," Raggedy Andy said as he and Raggedy Ann, Wamba the Witch, the kindly Ragman and little Buttons sat in the forest and looked toward the place where the fairy princess's castle had once stood.

"You folks stay here and I will walk over and see," the kindly Ragman said as he picked up his stout stick and crept through the bushes.

The Raggedys and Wamba the Witch watched the kindly Ragman as he walked up and down the path, trying to find a suitable place to enter the tangle of briars and thorns.

Finally the Ragman returned. "Mr. Loody told us that he had seen the three men go through the thorns," the Ragman said, "but there is no place where a person can possibly get through without an ax!"

"Perhaps if we walk around the tangle of thorns and briars, we shall find an entrance on the other side," Raggedy Ann suggested.

"Perhaps, but I doubt it very much," Wamba the Witch said. "I really believe that the three men who carried away our friend Teely Telly are in some way mixed up with the magic which made the fairy castle disappear. And, unless we are fortunate enough to discover the magically hidden entrance, we shall never rescue little Teely Telly!"

"Why don't you try using your magical charms, Wamba?" Raggedy Andy asked.

"Maybe, if we all get upon our magical hobbyhorses, we can ride right through the tangle of thorns and briars," Raggedy Ann suggested.

"I will try it," the kindly Ragman said as he reached for one of the hobbyhorses Raggedy Andy had stood against a tree. "There is no need for you folks to get scratched up unless I get through."

"If you can ride the hobbyhorse through, we will get upon ours and follow you," Wamba said.

The kindly Ragman led his magical hobbyhorse through the bushes to the path; then, when he had mounted, he called, "Gittyapp!" and rode the magical hobbyhorse straight toward the tangle of thorns with terrific force, but it was just like running against a springy wire fence.

The tough briars and thorns threw the hobbyhorse and the kindly Ragman far back into the underbrush, and when Wamba the Witch, Raggedy Ann and Raggedy Andy reached them, the kindly Ragman was just

54

getting to his feet and the hobbyhorse was hanging in the top branches of a low tree.

The clothing of the kindly Ragman was torn and his hands and face were scratched, but he smiled just the same. "I rode the magical hobbyhorse against the thorns as hard as he would go," he said, "but the thorns and briars are as tough as iron!"

Wamba the Witch took out her magical charms and rubbed them over the scratches on the kindly Ragman and immediately his wounds disappeared.

"I shall try again," the Ragman said. "One must never give up just because he does not succeed the first time." He laughed. "This time I shall try riding up in the air and over the briars and thorn trees!"

And without another word the Ragman lifted his magical hobbyhorse from the tree and mounted him. Again he rode toward the tangle, hoping that the hobby-horse would sail up in the air and over the thorns, but again the hobbyhorse and the kindly Ragman were sent sailing back in a heap.

"It won't work," the Ragman sighed as he rubbed his bruises. "I know I should not give up the second time, either, but really, I believe we shall not be able to ride our magical hobbyhorses through these magical thorns and briars."

"I just wonder!" Raggedy Andy mused half to himself.

"You just wonder what?" the Ragman asked when Wamba the Witch had again healed his scratches.

"Oh, nothing," Raggedy Andy replied. "I was just wondering. But it was too silly."

"Any idea you may have may be the right thing to do," Wamba the Witch said encouragingly. "Tell us what you wondered, Raggedy Andy."

"It was very silly," Raggedy Andy said sheepishly, "but it was this: I thought, seeing that the tangle of thorns and briars is magical and that whoever tries to get through will try with force, perhaps if we just walk up to the tangle careless-like and gently, we shall break the charm and walk right through! Now, wasn't that silly?" he asked.

"Why, I don't think it silly at all!" Wamba the Witch cried. "We will try it. Let us lead our magical hobbyhorses."

Wamba the Witch went first, then Raggedy Andy, then Raggedy Ann, then the kindly Ragman; Buttons, the puppy, brought up the rear.

Wamba the Witch walked leisurely up to the tangle of briars and thorns just as if there were none there and was surprised to find that she had walked six or eight feet into the tangle before the thorns held her back and she could go no farther. "Back out," Wamba said.

When all had safely backed out of the tangle, Wamba the Witch said, "Now, you see, Raggedy Andy, your idea was not so silly after all! And I shall tell you what I believe. We got just so far into this magical tangle because we thought we would, but just as soon as I began to think, 'Perhaps the thorns will stop us when we have reached the center,' then the thorns really did stop me. Now," she continued, "let us try blindfolding our eyes, so that we shall not see the briars and thorns, and let us each think that now we shall get through."

After each had tied a handkerchief about his eyes, Wamba the Witch caught hold of Raggedy Andy's hand, Raggedy Andy took the soft cottony hand of Raggedy Ann, and Raggedy Ann took the hand of the kindly Ragman.

"Now! Straight ahead!" Wamba the Witch cried as she walked right into the tangle of briars and thorns.

When they had walked for five minutes and Wamba could not feel the brambles and thorns brushing against her clothes, she stopped and took the handkerchief from her eyes. "Well, I declare!" she cried excitedly. "Will you look at this!"

When her friends hastily uncovered their eyes, they too gasped in amazement, for there before them stood the beautiful castle of the fairy princess, with its wonderful towers of pink and white marble reaching up almost to the clouds.

"Ha!" the kindly Ragman said. "The castle was not destroyed, as Loody thought, but has been hidden all these years by the magical tangle of briars and thorns. Now," he added, "the thing to consider is, how shall we get into the castle?"

This was not left long in doubt, for the kindly Ragman had hardly finished speaking when the drawbridge lowered with a great clanking of chains and a large man dressed in armor came galloping out toward them with his long lance pointed at our friends.

"Run!" Wamba the Witch cried as she lifted her skirts and ran for a large tree. Raggedy Andy caught hold of Raggedy Ann's hand and followed, almost dragging his sister in his haste.

The kindly Ragman, however, grasped his stout stick in his right hand and hopped upon his magical hobbyhorse. Very quietly he stood until the knight was almost upon him; then, with a touch of the rein, the Ragman sent his magical hobbyhorse to one side and out of the way of the knight's lance.

Time and again the knight charged, and time and again the kindly Ragman with a mocking cry rode to one side out of harm's way.

The knight's horse grew tired after charging so often and finally was brought to a stop a few feet from where the kindly Ragman sat upon his magical hobbyhorse. "Why don't you stand still and fight?" the knight cried as he raised the visor of his helmet.

"And why don't you move faster and fight?" the kindly Ragman said in response.

"Just as soon as my horse has rested, I shall ride you down," the knight cried, "and if you will stand still, I shall have you dangling from my spear in three shakes!"

"Then perhaps I should not give your horse time to rest," the Ragman said with a chuckle. And, as Raggedy Ann and Raggedy Andy and Wamba the Witch watched from behind the large tree, the kindly Ragman clicked to his magical hobbyhorse and rode full speed toward the knight.

As the Ragman rode toward him, the knight pointed his lance directly at the Ragman's breast. But the magical hobbyhorse obeyed every twitch of the rein, and just when it seemed that the Ragman was about to ride against the point of the lance, the magical hobbyhorse whirled to one side and carried the Ragman around the knight.

As he passed, the Ragman reached out and gave the knight a rap upon his steel helmet. The helmet rang loudly from the blow, which made the knight drop his lance.

As the kindly Ragman rode his magical hobbyhorse first on one side, then on the other, the knight did not know what to do, so he kept turning his horse until the poor creature became so dizzy he sat down.

Then the Ragman rode up to him, and as the knight swung his sword and missed, the Ragman's stout stick caught the knight's helmet and carried it from his head.

"Aha!" the Ragman cried. "Now we are even, and I shall show you a neat trick!" And making his magical hobbyhorse whirl to one side, the Ragman gave the knight a resounding whack upon the head which sent the knight spinning from his horse.

The Ragman rode his magical hobbyhorse up to the fallen knight and took his sword. Then, placing one foot upon the chest of the fallen knight, he pointed the sword at the knight's unprotected throat.

An Invisible Magician

The kindly Ragman proved himself more than a match for the knight who had ridden out of the magic castle to give him battle. While Wamba the Witch, Raggedy Ann and Andy, and little Buttons watched, the Ragman, with his stout stick, knocked the knight from his horse.

"Are there any more knights in the castle who will ride out here to fight with me?" the Ragman asked.

"There are a great many more knights inside, to be sure," the knight replied, "but I am certain they will be afraid to fight with you."

"Could you use your magic to heal the large bump on the knight's head?" the Ragman asked Wamba the Witch. And Wamba quickly healed it.

"Now that you have been so kind to me after you fought with me, I'll tell you a secret," the knight said.

"You must leave here just as soon as you can. Muggs the Magician is asleep and does not know you are here. If he should waken and find out, he would destroy you just like that!" And the knight snapped his fingers. "You see," he explained, "when Muggs the Magician goes to sleep, we dare not waken him. He has been asleep for four days and nights now and may waken at any time."

"Oh, that will be all right!" the Ragman said with a laugh. "When we tell Muggs the Magician our business, he will forget all about your letting us in."

"Well, if you really wish to see Muggs on business, then I suppose I must let you in. But I warn you to be very cautious. Muggs is easily angered."

The knight mounted his horse and, with our friends close beside him, led the way across the drawbridge and into the castle yard. The drawbridge was raised with a great clanking of chains.

It was truly a marvelous sight inside. There were great columns of snow-white marble. Rows of colored fountains threw a perfumed spray into the air.

"I can take you no farther," the knight said as his horse reached the foot of a great stairway. "I am afraid I have already brought you too far."

He left the Ragman, Wamba the Witch, the Raggedys, and Buttons, the puppy, standing at the foot of the stairs, undecided what to do or just where to go. Since no one came to meet them, the Ragman said, "Well, if there is no one to stop us, there is no reason why we should not look about. Perhaps we can find Muggs's sleeping place and waken him ourselves!"

"The knight evidently meant for us to go up this stairway," Wamba suggested, "so let us run up and look around."

But, when she and the Ragman started up the stairs, they were pushed back so violently that they tumbled against the rag dolls, and all fell to the floor in a heap. Then there sounded throughout the castle a great ringing of bells and the echoes of footsteps upon the marble floors. But our friends could see no one, even though the footsteps sounded close by and seemed to be running up the steps. Then, as they got to their feet and stood listening, a great voice sounded far above them somewhere in the castle: "Bring them here to me! I will teach them to wander unbidden into the castle of Muggs the Magician!"

Then our friends felt themselves grasped by invisible hands that half carried and half dragged them up the great stairway and into a great room. There stood a large throne carved of ivory and gold and inlaid with jade and other precious stones.

They were hurled to the floor, and a great voice coming from the empty throne made them shiver with fright: "Fools! Tell me what you wish before I destroy you!"

"We are in search of little Teely Telly, a pretty little friend of Raggedy Ann and Raggedy Andy," the Ragman said in a firm voice.

"Ah!" the great voice boomed. "I might have known it was something like that! Do not be surprised if you feel yourselves go up in smoke!"

"We shan't!" the Ragman said. "That is, kind Mister

Muggs, we shan't be surprised at all, for we hear that your magic is very powerful!"

"Aha!" the magician cried. "You are saying nice things in the hope that I shall let you go! But, never fear, I shall begin working my magic presently."

"I feel rather warm," the Ragman said. "But really, I believe that is caused by a warm glow of friendliness."

"Bah!" the great voice cried. And as our friends watched toward the sound of the voice, two large eyes appeared, then a long nose, then the rest of the face and body of Muggs the Magician.

"Now," Muggs cried as he rolled his eyes, "prepare to shrivel up into nothing." And with this, he waved a magic wand toward our friends and cried, "Slokus! Pokus! Shrivel up and turn into smoke!"

A Witch Defies a Magician

Wamba the Witch, the kindly Ragman, Raggedy Ann and Raggedy Andy stood before the throne of Muggs the Magician. Muggs was a fearsome sight as he rolled his large eyes and cried, "Slokus! Pokus! Shrivel up and turn into smoke!" And he waved his magic wand before him.

Raggedy Ann and Andy fully expected to have something happen to them. They did not know how it would feel to shrivel up into nothing but smoke, but they feared it would not be very comfortable. They held their breath while Muggs spoke. Then, as nothing strange happened to them, they each breathed easier.

"Now, what is the matter?" the magician cried as he saw that his magic did not work.

"Maybe your magic is not strong today on account of the damp weather we have been having," the Ragman suggested.

"It has never failed me before!" Muggs howled. "I'll try again."

He waved his magic wand before our friends again, and still not a thing happened.

"Maybe if you wait úntil tomorrow your magic will dry out, and it may work very well," the Ragman said.

"Please be quiet!" Muggs commanded. "How can I think when you chatter that way?"

"Try holding your magic wand in your left hand instead of your right hand," the Ragman said.

"I shall do nothing of the kind!" Muggs howled in a dismal tone. "Something has gone wrong with my magic, and I believe you are to blame!"

"I do not believe so," the Ragman said. "You see, Mr. Muggs, your magic will not work because we feel very friendly toward you. Now, if you would only try your magic and do something nice for us, I am certain it would work."

"Bah! In fact, two bahs!" Muggs cried. "I have never, never, done nice things for anyone, and I am too old to start now! I shall put you in prison and keep you there forever and ever!"

"We came to find little Teely Telly, Mr. Muggs," Raggedy Ann said, "and if you can help us find her, I am sure your magic will work nicely!"

"Now, then, will you please be quiet, you little rag doll? One reason why I want you to shrivel up into smoke is because I do not want you to rescue Teely Telly. Can't you understand that?"

"Oh, but we might be able to do something nice for

you if you would let us rescue little Teely Telly!" Raggedy Andy said, thinking of Teely Telly's magic.

"There is only one possible way for you ever to set
eyes upon Teely Telly again," Muggs said. "I would be
foolish to tell you how!"

Wamba the Witch, the kindly Ragman and the rag
dolls remained silent while Muggs the Magician rolled
his eyes. He seemed to be considering something.
Finally he said, "There is one thing I have always
wanted, and if you can get it for me, perhaps I shall let
you see little Teely Telly."

"What is it?" the Ragman wished to know.

"It's a carriage that runs without a horse pulling it," Muggs replied. Then, after considering a moment, he said, "I shall put you out of the castle and back into the woods where you came from. Then, if you can bring me the carriage, I will let you in again."

"That is fair enough!" the Ragman said, quite glad to escape from Muggs the Magician. "We will go right away!"

"Now what shall we do?" Raggedy Ann asked when they were outside again.

"Maybe I can make the carriage with my magic," Wamba the Witch said. But although she tried ever so hard, no carriage appeared. So, getting upon their magical hobbyhorses, our friends rode around the thicket until they came to a strange-looking house.

A cheery-looking fat man stood in the door and waved a friendly greeting to them. "Good morning!" Wamba said. "Do you know where we can find a horseless carriage?"

The fat man laughed. "Indeed I do! Right around in back of the house is an old one!" And he led the way and showed them a rickety old carriage. "I used to have a nice old horse," the fat man said, "but now I only have the carriage, so it is a horseless carriage now!"

"I'm afraid it is not what we are looking for," Wamba said, "but we thank you just the same!"

"Won't you come inside?" the fat man asked. "This is an inn, you know."

"We have no money," the Ragman said.

"My friend, that makes no difference!" The fat man laughed as he opened the door and waved them inside. "I never charge anything for anything I have here!"

Inside, our friends found a long counter with stools in front and a marble soda water fountain in back. "What flavors do you wish?" the fat man asked as he brought out five glasses. Each of our friends selected his favorite flavor, and the fat man made the sodas, plus one for himself. "I always like to be sociable," he chuckled, "so I have a soda with everyone who comes here."

They sat and talked and each had six sodas, for, or you no doubt have guessed, they were magical sodas, and you can easily drink six ice cream sodas if they are magical.

The kindly Ragman told the fat man why they were in the forest. When he had finished, the fat man said, "Perhaps you could pull the old rickety carriage through the thicket and fool old Muggs into thinking it is the one he wishes!"

"I'm afraid not." The Ragman sighed. "Muggs wanted one to ride in."

"Why not hitch one of your magical hobbyhorses to it?" the fat man suggested.

"Whee!" Wamba the Witch cried. "That is just what we had better do!"

The fat man found some pieces of harness and straps and rope. With these, Wamba's magical hobbyhorse was soon hitched to the rickety carriage. They thanked the fat man for the carriage and the sodas, and after they had all climbed into the carriage, they drove it around the thicket to where they had come out from the magical castle.

All closed their eyes as Wamba the Witch drove the magical hobbyhorse and the rickety carriage right through the briars and thorns and into the large hall of the castle. "Here we are!" she cried to the invisible people she knew were all about them.

Presently they heard the loud voice of Muggs crying, "Bring them here immediately!" And the magical hobbyhorse, the rickety carriage and our friends were pulled and pushed up the great stairway into the large room where Muggs the Magician sat upon his throne.

"What do you mean by bringing that rickety carriage here?" he howled in such a loud voice that Raggedy Ann shivered.

"Because you wanted a horseless carriage, and here it is!" Wamba the Witch replied.

"I wouldn't have such a rickety, crazy-looking thing!" Muggs howled. "And besides, it isn't a horseless carriage when you have a horse hitched to it!"

"But it isn't a real horse!" Wamba said.

"Silly!" Muggs howled. "Can't I see that? I won't have it! Take it away! Take it away!"

Wamba the Witch hopped out of the carriage and ran up to Muggs, shaking her finger in his face. "Now, Mister Muggs," she cried, "you promised us that if we brought you a horseless carriage, you would let us see Teely Telly!"

"Ha, ha! I've changed my mind!" Muggs howled. "I shall not let you see Teely Telly at all!"

"Then you are a fibber and a very wicked creature!" Wamba cried. And before she stopped to think, she boxed the magician's ear so hard, his head flew from his body and rolled all the way across the room.

Some Adventures with Magic

When Wamba the Witch jumped from the rickety buggy and boxed the ears of Muggs the Magician, Raggedy Ann, Raggedy Andy and the kindly Ragman held their breath, for what was their surprise to see the large head of Muggs go rolling across the floor. Sitting upon the throne was a little weazened, wrinkled old man.

"Aha!" Wamba cried, catching the little old man by the ear and shaking him until his teeth rattled. "So this is where you have been hiding all these years!"

"Long live the queen!" all the voices of the invisible people cried.

"Be quiet!" Wamba the Witch cried as she held up her hand. "I am not your queen, any more than this" —pointing to the little old man—"humbug was a magician. He is my husband who ran away from home

75

years ago when I sent him to the grocery for a loaf of bread and some dill pickles."

Wamba the Witch looked all about her for a while and then said, "I want to know why all of the people here are invisible."

Then the voice of a woman spoke and said, "We do not know why we are invisible. We can see each other and we can see you, and we feel no different than we did before we were made invisible."

"Then," Wamba cried as she brought out her magic charms, "I shall see if I can make you visible!"

She placed the magic charms in a circle and sprinkled

some powder from a tiny blue bottle into a little tin dish; this she lighted, and as the thread of smoke curled up into the air, Wamba danced about the circle and sang a magic song. And as the Raggedys and the kindly Ragman watched, they saw the faces and then the bodies of the people of the castle appear.

"I am not your queen," Wamba the Witch repeated, "nor do I wish to be a queen. But I do wish to know just what has been going on in this castle. Can you tell me anything about it?" she asked a lovely young lady standing near the throne.

"I can perhaps tell you as much as any of us know,"

the lady replied. "A few years ago, something happened. None of us know just what it was, because none of us can remember farther back than that certain day. It was just as if all of us had been born full-grown that day, and here we have had to stay, for we found that we could not pass beyond the dense thicket of briars and thorns."

"Hmmm!" Wamba the Witch mused. "Then Muggs must know all about it. Where is he?"

"He has gone!" Raggedy Ann said. "I saw the Ragman start after him."

"We must find him at once if we wish to get to the bottom of all this magic," Wamba said. Then she asked the lovely young lady, "Do you know where little Teely Telly and the three men are?"

"No," the lovely lady replied. "I do not know where she is or who she is."

At this moment up came the Ragman, followed by a number of men and leading Muggs.

Wamba the Witch motioned for Muggs to stand in front of her. "Now, Muggs," she said in a stern voice, "I want you to tell me where little Teely Telly is."

"Honest, Wamba, I don't know," Muggs replied.

"Perhaps Muggs has forgotten everything, too," Raggedy Ann whispered to Wamba.

"Perhaps he has," Wamba agreed. "I will soon find out." She again took the charms from her handbag and placed them in a circle around Muggs, then again she danced and sang another magic song.

As she danced, Raggedy Ann and Raggedy Andy

could see a change come over the face of Muggs. He appeared to be coming out of a deep sleep, and as he rubbed his eyes, he looked about him in astonishment.

"Where am I?" he asked. "Oh! Now I remember, my dear. I started to the grocery, just as you told me to, but when I came to the thicket of briars and thorns, I saw a pretty white rabbit hopping along a path, so I followed the little white rabbit until I came to the courtyard here and saw all the people standing about fast asleep!"

"Just like the sleeping beauty in the fairy tale!" Raggedy Ann cried.

"Just that way, my dear," Muggs said. "I walked inside the castle and here to the throne room, where I saw, sitting in this seat, a man with long white whiskers, also fast asleep. I do not know why I did it, but when I saw a magic wand in his hand, I took it from him. Immediately he awakened and with a loud howl jumped at me. I ran as fast as I could, with him right after me. Through one room and into another, we ran all over the castle until we came to a small room. I started to jump through the door, but instead I slipped to my hands and knees, and he was so close to me he could not stop in time. He tripped over me and fell. His head struck the edge of the door and this knocked him silly, I guess, for it was easy for me to drag him into the small room, tie his hands and feet and lock the door until I had time to rest and think things over.

"Well, sir," Muggs continued, "when I went back through the castle, I found a book of magic. In my searching I discovered that this old man with the long whiskers was an evil magician who had brought the

80

sleeping magic upon everyone in the castle. I read the magic book and tried to discover just how to work magic so that I could awaken the people. But though I tried ever so hard, I only succeeded in making them invisible when I did awaken them. And, as it was I who had awakened them, they thought that I was really the magician and they readily obeyed my wishes."

"Then will you see if you can make heads or tails of it, Raggedy Andy," Wamba the Witch said. But when Raggedy Andy looked at the printing in the magic book, he knew no more than Wamba.

"Perhaps if you used the magician's wand along with your other magical charms, you might discover how to read the book," the kindly Ragman said.

"I shall try it," Wamba agreed as she took her magic charms from her handbag and placed them in front of the throne. After she had sprinkled the magic powder upon a small flame and danced about the charms, Wamba again read in the magic book. "Aha!" she cried. "That was just the thing to do! Now I can read every-thing just as easy as anything!"

After a while Wamba looked up from the magic book and said, "Now, none of you can possibly guess what I have just read! And I am certain that when I work some of the magic, you will all be surprised. The first thing to do, however, is to have the real magician brought here. And you must take great care that he does not escape. For, should he escape, we may never be able to solve the riddle of the magic castle and the sleeping people and little Teely Telly."

Teely Telly Is Found at Last

Wamba the Witch, the Raggedys and the kindly Ragman slept well in the magical castle. When they awakened in the morning they wondered what the day would
bring in the way of surprises.

Immediately after breakfast, Wamba called everyone
to the throne room and said, "We still do not know why
all of you have lost your memories. Perhaps if you will
bring me the magic book you found, Muggs, and the
magic wand of the real magician, I may discover something."

Muggs hastened to bring the magic book and the
magic wand. He handed them to Wamba, his wife. "I
never could seem to make the magic wand work magic
very well," he said.

Wamba did not reply immediately; she was reading
in the magic book. At last she said, "I cannot make

heads or tails of the directions for working magic. The words are jumbled up in every direction and make no sense when they are read right across the page!"

"Perhaps they are printed in some kind of code," Raggedy Andy suggested.

The kindly Ragman and ten of the courtiers went with Muggs to where he had confined the magician. "I had him put in chains and locked to a large iron ring in the floor," Muggs told the Ragman.

When the men reached the room in which Muggs had confined the real magician, they discovered that the chains were lying upon the floor but the magician had disappeared. "Ha!" Muggs cried as he held his head. "Someone has helped the magician to escape, that is certain. I had him chained to the floor so well, he never, never could have unfastened himself. Now what shall we do? Wamba will be so angry!"

Wamba was not angry with Muggs, though she was disappointed. "As you say, Muggs," Wamba said, "someone within this castle has helped the magician to escape, and we must discover who it is!"

So she again worked her magic with the magic powder and waved the magician's magic wand. There was a sound as loud as thunder all through the castle. Everyone thought the walls would tumble in, they shook and rattled so.

When the noise ceased, Wamba said, "The noise we heard was my magic clashing with his. It is just like two thunderstorms coming together. Now, do not be frightened, for if the magician's magic had been stronger than mine, he would be standing here now, making us all pay for what we are trying to do to him! I shall try again!"

Again Wamba worked her magic and waved the magician's wand, and this time the noise was not so loud. Three times Wamba did the same thing, until at last there was no noise at all. "I believe," she cried, "that I have conquered the magician and that he has been driven from the magical castle and will not bother us again!"

"Do you know what I believe, Wamba?" the Ragman asked. "I believe that the magician had someone inside the castle who helped him, and that the three men who carried away little Teely Telly must know something about it. Why not bring them here and question them?"

"I know what I shall do," Wamba said. "I have a magic ball which rolls along in search of things. It used to come in very handy when Muggs dropped a collar button on the floor and it rolled away and hid. We can follow the magic ball and discover where the three men are hiding. We must watch, though, for they will try to escape and may fight very hard."

Wamba took the little magic ball from her purse and, after saying a few magic words above it, placed it on the floor. Immediately the magic ball began moving.

The magic ball went from the top of the castle to the bottom and finally rolled slowly down into the basement, deep, deep below the ground. Here it turned into a dark passageway and came to rest at a door.

When the Ragman opened the door, to everyone's surprise there was Buttons, the little dog, fast asleep, lying against another door.

"Little Buttons!" Raggedy Ann and Raggedy Andy cried as they ran forward. "We had forgotten you! Wake up! Wake up!" But Buttons could not be awakened until Wamba the Witch worked her magic upon him. Then he barked and wagged his tail and jumped against the second door as much as to say, "They are in there! I followed their scent as soon as I got into the castle, and I stayed by the door so they could not get out!"

And when the kindly Ragman opened the door, sure enough, there sat the three large, fierce-looking men, fast asleep, and nearby in a glass box lay little Teely Telly.

Buttons Finds the Real Magician

"Aha!" cried Wamba the Witch when she and her friends discovered the three men fast asleep down in the basement of the magical castle. "These are the three men who carried away little Teely Telly! And," Wamba cried as she pointed to a glass box at one side, "there lies Teely Telly!"

The three fierce men, still fast asleep, with little Teely Telly in the glass box, were carried to the throne room. Then again Wamba got out her magic wand and read from the magician's great book of magic.

When Wamba had worked her magic, the three men yawned and stretched and awakened.

"Why did you capture little Teely Telly and bring her here?" Wamba asked.

"The magician commanded us to bring her here," one of the men replied.

"Did you help the magician to escape from his chains?" Wamba asked.

"Yes," the man answered. "He promised us that if we helped him escape he would reward us."

"Now, I do not wish to ask you so many questions," Wamba said, pointing her wand straight at the man's red nose, "so you start at the beginning and tell me exactly what happened. And be careful! If I find that you do not tell me the truth, I shall turn you into a hoppy toad, just as I have done to the magician. Now begin."

The man could feel cold chills run up his spine, so with a frightened glance at his companions he said, "A short time ago, we three found a way to come through the thicket of thorns and briars and to enter this castle. We took great care that we should not be discovered until we had come to the room where the magician was chained to the floor. We told him that we would unfasten his chains if he would give us a chest of gold so that we could buy a ship and become pirates. This he promised us, so we filed his chains and set him free. Then he told us that if we would go to the little home of Teely Telly and bring her here to the castle, he would not only give us the chest of gold, but would, with his magic, make us a fine ship. So we set out and brought little Teely Telly here."

"Did the magician give you the chest of gold?" Wamba asked.

"Yes," one man replied. "When we went after little Teely Telly, we took it with us and hid it in the woods."

"I shall never use a penny of the gold," one of the

fierce-looking men said. "Nor I, either," the other two chimed in.

The one who had told Wamba the story then spoke: "Since we have awakened from our sleep here, I am certain that we do not care to become pirates. I shall never do another unkind deed as long as I live."

"I believe you when you say you will never do an unkind deed from now on," Wamba the Witch said, "so I shall let you go." Then she ordered the ropes taken from the men so that they could stand up and stretch themselves. "Now, if I were you," Wamba said, "I would take the chest of gold the magician gave you and I would see just how much happiness I could make with it."

"Yes," one of the men said, "we will take it and build an orphanage where we can make hundreds of children happy."

"That is a very good idea," Wamba said. "I am certain that you will all get a lot of pleasure out of it."

When the three men had gone, Wamba said, "Now, I shall work my magic upon little Teely Telly and awaken her. Everyone remain quiet, please."

So presently little Teely Telly opened her lovely eyes and then yawned and sat up in the glass box. She was as surprised as the three men had been to see so many persons about her. But Raggedy Ann ran to Teely Telly and threw her cotton-stuffed arms about her.

"I am happy to see you, Raggedy Ann! And you too, Raggedy Andy," little Teely Telly said in her soft, silvery tone, "but please tell me where I am and what all these people are doing here."

Raggedy Ann helped little Teely Telly from the glass box. Then she introduced Teely Telly to Wamba the Witch and to the kindly Ragman. Raggedy Ann told her everything that had happened since she and Raggedy Andy had arrived at the castle.

Just as Raggedy Ann finished her story, little Buttons came running to the throne and placed before Wamba a large hoppy toad. Then he barked loudly and jumped up and down as if trying to tell Wamba something.

"He's trying to tell you that this hoppy toad is the magician, Wamba," Raggedy Andy said, "I'll bet a nickel."

"I wonder if it can be?" Wamba said, half to herself. "I was only fooling, you know, when I said I had changed the magician into a hoppy toad."

The Ragman laughed. "Well, perhaps you had the wand in your hand when you said it, and that made the real magic happen. How can you tell, Wamba?"

"I can easily discover that with my magic," Wamba said as she drew a circle about the hoppy toad. "Now, Mister Hoppy Toad," she said as she touched him with the magic wand, "if you are the wicked magician, stand up on your hind feet." And sure enough the hoppy toad stood up.

There stood the tall magician, his long white beard touching the ground and his knees trembling so violently he could scarcely stand up.

The Magic of Happiness

With a touch of her magic wand, Wamba the Witch had changed the magician from a hoppy toad into his true form. And there he stood in his long black cloak and his white beard, shaking with fright. The magician knew very well that Wamba the Witch with her good magic was more than a match for his selfish magic, and he was much afraid that Wamba would punish him.

"Now, Mister Magician," Wamba said, and her voice was kind but firm, "unless you wish to be changed into a hoppy toad again, you must tell us exactly why you had the three men capture lovely little Teely Telly and bring her here to your castle."

The magician wiggled and twisted about just as a small boy does when he is ashamed of himself. Then he finally said, "I see that it is no use trying to tell you a fib, Wamba, so I shall tell you everything.

"A long, long time ago," the magician said, "this

91

lovely castle was owned by a very good king and queen who were dearly loved by everybody. But one day when the king and queen went on a long journey to visit relatives, I thought to myself, 'It would be very nice for me if I owned this castle and all the people.' So, I studied my book of magic, and with my charms I had a great storm sweep over the land. Then I caused all of the people to go to sleep, just as I have read they did in the story about Sleeping Beauty. When all the people had gone to sleep, I caused the thicket of briars and thorns to grow up around the castle so that no one could get in here.

"The king and queen had a beautiful daughter whom they loved very dearly. But, as I was afraid the daughter would grow up and be able to work good magic, I had her carried away into the forest. For years and years I thought the princess had gone for good. But one day I discovered that she was still alive and that she was working her good magic to help the little creatures who live in the forest. So, being afraid that someday she would learn of what I had done, I sent three men to capture her and bring her here. With my magic I put her to sleep and would have kept her in the glass box for hundreds of years if you had not come along and spoiled my plans."

"Oh! Goody! Goody!" Raggedy Ann cried. "Little Teely Telly is a real-for-sure fairy princess!"

"Isn't that lovely!" the kindly Ragman said. "Anyone can easily see that to be true!"

As the kindly Ragman spoke, the tall magician turned and looked at him, and if he had not caught hold of the throne, the magician would have fallen down, his knees shook so hard.

"Now, Mister Magician," Wamba cried as she pointed the wand at him, "what is the trouble? Why do your knees shake? Tell us!"

The magician was very frightened, and it was quite a while before he could find his voice. Then he said, "I worked my magic upon the king and queen, but I never discovered what became of them. Now I know that this kindly Ragman is . . . is . . . is . . ." And the magician's voice grew fainter and fainter as his knees shook.

"Ha!" Wamba cried. "Speak up, old Mister Magician, or I shall turn you back into a hoppy toad. Is the kindly Ragman the king?"

"Yes," the magician replied in a weak voice. "He is Teely Telly's father, and now that he knows it, I am afraid!"

Wamba pointed her wand at the kindly Ragman and spoke a few magic words. The Ragman rubbed his eyes and looked about him in a bewildered way. Then, seeing little Teely Telly standing with her arm about Raggedy Ann, he ran and took her in his arms.

"Now, Mister Magician," Wamba cried, "doesn't it make you feel small and ashamed to think of the years of unhappiness you have caused these good people? Well, I should think it would!"

The magician nodded his head and then said, "It is only just now, this very minute, that I am able to know where the queen is! So, Wamba, if you will work your magic, you can easily bring her here." Wamba the

Witch waved the magic wand and spoke the magic words and into the throne room walked a lovely old lady.

"Hooray!" cried Raggedy Ann and Raggedy Andy.

Then the magician said, "You are the queen and the Ragman is the king and Teely Telly is the princess! If Wamba will work her magic, I am sure you will all take your real shapes."

So Wamba waved her magic wand, and the kind old wrinkled face of the Ragman changed, and the sweet old face of the lady changed, and there they stood just as they had looked when they had left the castle years and years before. So the queen and the king took turns hugging Princess Teely Telly and laughed and cried with joy.

The old magician was silent for a moment as he brushed a tear from his eye. "I am so sorry that I was so mean and selfish," he said. "I wish I could undo all the sorrow and unhappiness I have caused you all these years."

"Perhaps," the king who had been the kindly Ragman suggested, "perhaps with your magic you can make us all forget. Perhaps you can work the magic so that none of us will remember that you caused us any unhappiness. Could you do that?"

"I should like to try," the magician said. "And, if I may do that, I am certain that I shall be the happiest person here!"

So, taking the large magic book and the magic charms, the magician pointed the magic wand to each point of the compass and spoke some magic words. When he had finished speaking, there was a sound as of many musicians playing softly on beautiful instruments, and all those in the great magic castle forgot that anything strange had ever befallen them. They laughed and talked together just as if they were having a lovely party, and neither the king who had been the Ragman, nor the queen, nor Wamba the Witch, nor Muggs, nor Princess Teely Telly ever once remembered that they had had such remarkable adventures as have here been told you.

And, if it had not been for the magician not forgetting, perhaps this might not have been told. Anyway,

the magician took good care that never again would he work magic which might cause anyone a moment's displeasure or unhappiness, and that is why, should you be fortunate enough to visit the magic castle of Princess Teely Telly, you would be received with love and unselfish friendliness.

For, those who really and truly have the magic of love in their hearts are filled with a sunny happiness which they always wish to share with those about them. So, the magical castle is always filled with the sunshine of happiness.

*　　*　　*　　*

"Now wasn't that a nice adventure?" said Raggedy Ann to Raggedy Andy, when the two rag dolls had returned to the packing case doll house in Marcella's backyard.

"Yes, indeed it was, Raggedy Ann," said Raggedy Andy. And they both smiled soft, cottony smiles and snuggled down in just the same positions that Marcella had left them before she went away. Then they waited quietly for their little mistress to come home again.